For everyone who hopes to make a difference,
let Spirit, Opportunity, and Curiosity light the way!
—SLH

To my five pets, the best friends to share adventures with.
—EP

Selected Bibliography

"Asteroid Belt Facts: Interesting Facts about the Asteroid Belt." The Planets. Accessed July 3, 2019. https://theplanets.org/asteroid-belt/.

"Curiosity Rover Mission Overview." NASA. Accessed June 29, 2019. https://mars.nasa.gov/msl/mission/overview/.

Loff, Sarah. "Mars Pathfinder Overview." NASA. June 23, 2017. Accessed July 2, 2019. https://www.nasa.gov/mission_pages/pathfinder/overview.

"Mars 2020 Mission Overview." NASA. Accessed June 30, 2019. https://mars.nasa.gov/mars2020/mission/overview/.

"Mars Exploration Rover—Opportunity." NASA. Accessed July 1, 2019. https://www.jpl.nasa.gov/missions/details.php?id=5909.

"Mars Exploration Rovers." NASA. Accessed July 18, 2019. https://mars.nasa.gov/programmissions/missions/past/2003/.

"Step-by-Step Guide to Entry, Descent, and Landing." NASA. Accessed July 1, 2019. https://mars.nasa.gov/mer/mission/timeline/edl/steps/.

"Planets." NASA. April 10, 2019. Accessed July 2, 2019. https://solarsystem.nasa.gov/planets/overview/.

Copyright © 2020 by Sourcebooks
Text by Susanna Leonard Hill
Illustrations by Elisa Paganelli
Cover and internal design © 2020 by Sourcebooks
Internal images © NASA/JPL-Caltech,
NASA/JPL/Malin Space Science Systems,
NASA/JPL/Cornell University/Maas Digital

Sourcebooks and the colophon are registered trademarks of Sourcebooks.

All rights reserved.

All brand names and product names used in this book are trademarks, registered trademarks, or trade names of their respective holders. Sourcebooks is not associated with any product or vendor in this book.

All book illustrations have been sketched and colored in Photoshop with a Wacom Intuos tablet.

Published by Sourcebooks Wonderland, an imprint of Sourcebooks Kids
P.O. Box 4410, Naperville, Illinois 60567-4410
(630) 961-3900
sourcebookskids.com

Library of Congress Cataloging-in-Publication Data is on file with the publisher.

Source of Production: Wing King Tong Paper Products Co. Ltd., Shenzhen, Guangdong Province, China
Date of Production: February 2020
Run Number: 5017350

Printed and bound in China.
WKT 10 9 8 7 6 5 4 3 2 1

MARS' FIRST FRIENDS

From the *New York Times*
Bestselling Team
★ Susanna Leonard Hill
and Elisa Paganelli

sourcebooks
wonderland

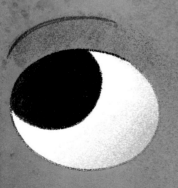

In a sky full of stars, Mars glowed fiery red.
   He longed for someone to have adventures with,
   discover new things with,
   laugh, and share secrets with,
   ...just to *be* with.
   Yes, he was one of eight in his solar system family,
but no one ever had time for him.

Mars was sad.
And bored.
And lonely.

So Mars went to the Sun.

"Dad," he said. "Could I please have a pet of my own? A friend I can always play with?"

But the Sun pointed out that their family already had a pet. Pluto!

"Neptune and Uranus keep Pluto all to themselves," complained Mars. "They stay way out where it's really cold, and it's too far for me to go by myself. I want my *own* pet."

The Sun sighed. "A pet is a big responsibility," he said.
"It's not all fun, and someone has to keep it in orbit."

Mars promised he would love and care for it, but the Sun would not be moved.

"You have seven siblings," he said firmly. "You can play with one of them."

Mars sighed and set out
in search of a playmate.

"Hey, Saturn," he greeted his sister.
"Can I do hoop-da-loops with you?"

But Saturn preferred to swing her rings alone.

Disappointed but determined, Mars headed for Jupiter.
"How about a little hide-and-seek?" he asked.

But Jupiter was too busy juggling his many moons.
He just didn't have time.

Mars had high hopes for a game with Earth.
He was closest to her, after all.

"I'd like to, Mars," said Earth with a yawn, "but just as I put half the humans to bed, the other half wake up. I'm so tired. Maybe later..."

Next, Mars approached his sister, Venus.
"Are you feeling up for a game?" Mars asked.

"I don't think so, Red," said Venus. "My temperature is so high, I think I just need to rest a bit."

Mars didn't bother asking Mercury. He was too young for games and always stayed by the Sun's side.
"I told you, Dad," said Mars, dispirited. "No one will play."

But wait!
What's over there?

Something was coming!
Two little spacecrafts hurtled into Mars' atmosphere at twelve thousand miles per hour, glowing like embers as hot as the Sun.

They came closer and closer!

Then the pieces that had kept them safe and snug for millions of miles dropped away in stages.

As the little crafts' parachutes popped out to slow them for landing, Mars wondered what they could be.

"What was that?" Mars asked as a lander thumped down on his surface. It bumped and bounced, tipped and tumbled, until it drifted to a stop in a cloud of ruby dust.

And soon the other would do the same.

"These are for me?"
he wondered aloud.

As the airbags fell away, two rovers from Earth emerged. Mars' heart skipped with excitement. Could they become his new best friends? Would he have someone to play with after all?

"Pets!" he exclaimed. "Not just one, but TWO! Thank you, Earth!" he shouted to his sister. "The whole family thought you'd like them, " said Earth.

The rovers raced about, exploring their new home. After the long journey, they were eager to play! Spirit and Opportunity were interested in everything, and Mars laughed at how curious they were.

It tickled when they roamed in and out of his craters.

He thought it was funny that they liked to collect rocks.

They played together in a red dust storm he sent out.

Mars had never had so much fun.

He curled up that night with Spirit and Opportunity
snuggled close.

"I promise I'll give you a good home, always," Mars
whispered to his new pets. "The very best!"

And who knows? he thought as he drifted off to sleep. Maybe more pets would come his way in the future...

Our Solar System

Phew! It's hot.

People call me Red!

Mercury
* Terrestrial planet
* 43.25 million miles from the Sun
* Only a tiny bit larger than Earth's Moon!

Venus
* Terrestrial planet
* 70 million miles from the Sun
* Its surface is 900 degrees Fahrenheit!

Earth
* Terrestrial planet
* 94.5 million miles from the Sun
* The perfect environment for life to call home!

Mars
* Terrestrial planet
* 153.5 million miles from the Sun
* A Martian year is 687 days on Earth!

Jupiter
* Gas giant
* 491.8 million miles from the Sun
* Has more than 75 moons!

Spiraling around the Milky Way at nearly 515,000 miles per hour, the solar system that we call home is a wondrous place! Made up of eight planets, a handful of dwarf planets like Pluto, more than 150 moons, and countless asteroids, comets, and meteoroids, the solar system formed nearly 4.5 billion years ago from a cosmic recipe of interstellar gas and dust clouds.

Over time, the eight amazing planets in the solar system gathered from stardust and space rock and began to orbit our Sun. **Mercury** is the smallest planet and the closest to the Sun, but still not quite as hot as **Venus**, which has a dense atmosphere that traps every bit of heat it can.

Earth is our planet, and the only one in the solar system that we know supports life. The fourth planet, **Mars**, is extra-special to this book (we'll get to him soon), and is separated from the fifth planet, Jupiter, by a large asteroid belt. **Jupiter** is a gas giant and bigger than all the other planets put together! **Saturn** is the sixth, and has thousands of beautiful, icy rings. **Uranus** is an ice giant with fewer rings than its neighbor, Saturn, and has a swirling blue atmosphere. **Neptune** is the furthest planet from the Sun, making it all the harder to learn about, but we do know it's the coldest and windiest!

Saturn

* Gas giant
* 934.1 million miles from the Sun
* Has seven gorgeous groups of rings!

Uranus

* Ice giant
* 1.8 billion miles from the Sun
* Smells like rotten eggs!

Neptune

* Ice giant
* 2.75 billion miles from the Sun
* The only planet not visible with the naked eye!

Pluto

* Dwarf planet
* 3.1 billion miles from the Sun
* Has a heart-shaped glacier bigger than Texas!

The Little Red Planet

Next to Earth and the Moon, Mars is the most visited and explored place in our solar system. A terrestrial planet (meaning it's made of rocks and metals, with a tough outer shell), the dusty, red-orange planet lies only 153.5 million miles from the Sun, and only about 60 million miles from our home! Though Mars has no atmosphere now and looks much like a desert here on Earth, scientists believe that it was once a warm, wet planet that may have even supported life of its own billions of years ago. Visits to our brother planet have revealed amazing structures on the Martian surface like polar ice caps, craters, deep canyons, and inactive volcanoes. All of these discoveries help us rebuild the history of Mars in order to better understand it, and perhaps one day send astronauts to visit it firsthand!

Image of Mars from NASA's Jet Propulsion Laboratory

Mission to Mars

The Mars Rover Program

NASA (National Aeronautics and Space Administration) was established July 29, 1958, as part of the U.S. government and is in charge of science and technology related to airplanes and space. From satellites and spaceships, to landers and probes, NASA does it all! One of NASA's most popular and long-lasting programs is the Mars Rover program, which is designed to explore Mars with different rovers—or mobile exploration robots—and gather important information for scientists. NASA hopes to uncover the mysteries of Mars by learning about its formation and evolution as a planet, its geological history, and if it hosted biological life; and to someday pave the way for future human exploration.

Full-scale models of three generations of NASA Mars rovers show the increase in size from the Sojourner rover of the Mars Pathfinder project (center), to the twin Mars Exploration Rovers Spirit and Opportunity (left), to the Curiosity rover (right).

Sojourner

The Mars Pathfinder mission landed a small test rover named Sojourner on the Martian surface on July 4, 1997. It was only ever intended to demonstrate how NASA might successfully deliver a rover to Mars. Against all odds, Pathfinder delivered Sojourner successfully, and the test rover actually gathered and delivered some of the most astounding information! From where it touched down in an ancient flood plain, Sojourner collected and transmitted nearly 2.3 billion bits of information, 16,500 pictures, and 15 sets of soil and rock analysis. After only a short visit, Sojourner stopped transmitting on September 27, 1997, having paved the way for NASA to send future exploration rovers to Mars.

Out-of-this-World Facts!

* Mars is named after the Roman god of war, but to different people in history, it was also called Ares, "fire star," and "the red one."

* Despite the big differences in volume, Mars and Earth have nearly the same amount of landmass! This is because of Earth's many oceans, which cover nearly 70% of its surface.

* On Mars, you can jump three times higher than on Earth! That's because the surface gravity on Mars is only about 35% of what it is on Earth.

* Mars boasts the tallest known mountain in the solar system, named Olympus Mons. The mountain stands over 21 kilometers high. That's over twice the size of Mount Everest!

Spirit and Opportunity

Launched in summer 2003, Mars' first real "pets," the twin Spirit and Opportunity rovers, were sent as a pair to explore Mars and its history, and to seek out signs of ancient life. In January 2004, Spirit landed first, with a combination of parachutes and inflatable airbags (that looked like a bunch of grapes!) to make sure it touched down safely. Spirit went on to uncover the first hard evidence that Mars had once been a wet, warm planet—the kind that astronauts say could have supported life! Additionally, recordings and measurements taken by Spirit helped NASA understand the phenomenon of Martian wind, which had puzzled them for years. Opportunity reached Mars second, with the same type of landing as Spirit. While exploring the Martian surface, Opportunity collected data that confirmed Mars' past potential for life, including information which showed that Mars may have had large seas at one point! Both Spirit and Opportunity carried out their missions for far longer than NASA scientists had hoped, working tirelessly to send home key information about Mars.

Curiosity

Landing on August 5, 2012, Curiosity is the most recent rover NASA sent to Mars. As part of NASA's Mars Science Laboratory mission, it was designed to test Mars' future "habitability," or whether the planet can sustain small forms of life known as microbes. To carry out this mission, Curiosity was built with the most advanced tools and technology, allowing the rover to analyze climate, geology, chemistry, and ancient environments. Curiosity is still active and also far more mobile than past rovers, capable of traveling almost 30 meters per hour with its cutting-edge electrical generator.

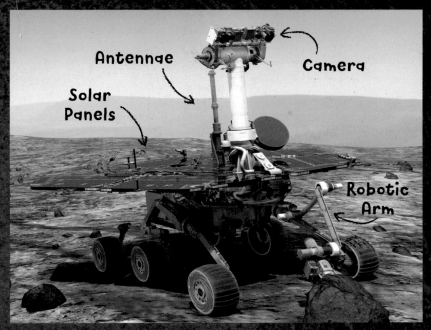

Spirit/Opportunity rover diagram

Scientists hope that data from Curiosity's mission might one day help us create habitable colonies on the Martian surface. Curiosity continues to roam Mars and collect vital information to send back to Earth.

What's Next?

NASA is continuing its program with another planned rover for Mars! This new pet will help provide the next step for understanding Mars' history and potential to sustain life. Unlike its predecessors, the rover will be equipped with a drill intended to retrieve samples from beneath the Martian surface, hopefully uncovering evidence of ancient microbial life. Unlike earlier missions, the rover is designed to collect and protect those samples so that future missions to the surface may recover them—and return them to Earth. This rover mission will use lessons learned from Sojourner, Spirit, Opportunity, and Curiosity to take the next step in NASA's exploration of Mars!